For my little Wolf cub, whose long winter slumber
inside of me helped inspire this story.

A special thankyou to Owlkids Books for helping
shape this wonderful project; to the Schleifenbaum
family and Haliburton Forest Wolf Centre staff,
who allowed me to observe and sketch their
wolves, and who showed me photo archives
and gave me detailed descriptions of the wolves'
behavior at rest, play, and feeding time; and to the
Ontario Arts Council for their generous gift of a
Writers' Reserve grant.

This book would not have been possible without
everyone's cooperation!

The Wolf~Birds

by Willow Dawson

Owlkids Books

Deep in the wild winter wood,
when the snow falls and
the icy winds blow,

two hungry ravens huddle
in wait for their next meal.

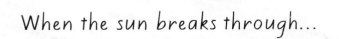

When the sun breaks through...

the two birds dig for caches
lost under the fresh, white flakes.

They search low and they search high until they hear a familiar sound... the sound of hungry wolves!

Past the forest line and up over the snow, four wolves are on the hunt.

But just when their meal
is within reach...

...their luck takes a tumbling turn.

Three wolves must say goodbye...

...and continue their search for food.

They travel to a high place
and see how winter stretches wide.

They sniff the chilly air and
inspect the cold ground below.
Then they hear a familiar sound...

Two birds dip their wings and cry out.
Three wolves follow.

Between aspen trunks stripped cold and bare, a starving deer favors an injured leg.

Out creep the wolves to begin their next chase.

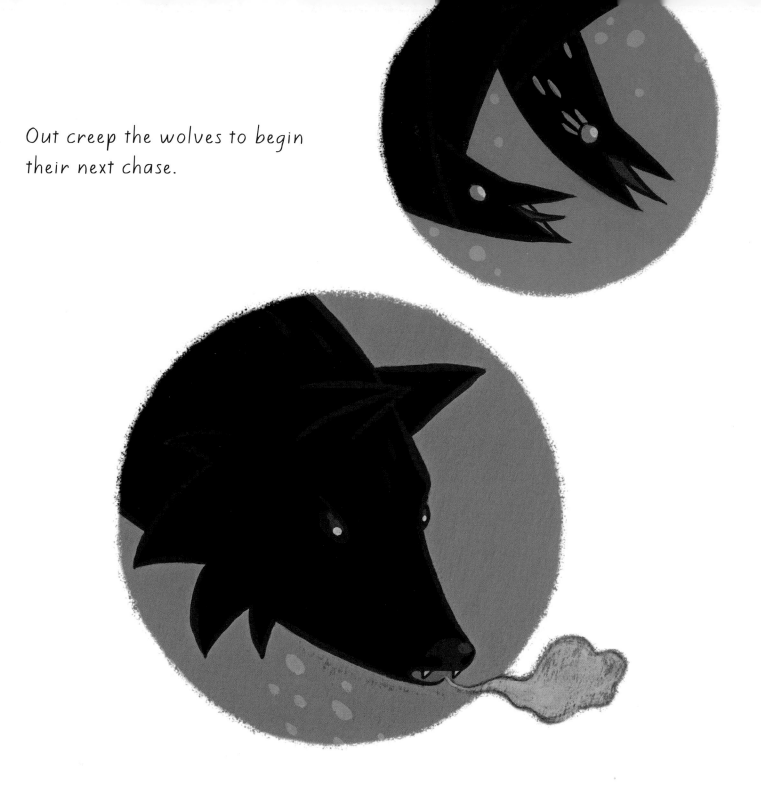

In the wild winter wood...

...one animal's life helps many others live.

From strongest to smallest, everyone feasts in turn, filling bellies and beaks.

Resting,

playing,

caching treats.

Stretching, then turning toward home.

Trundling over a snowy hill,
down to a warm den.

Gliding through the treetops,
up to a high nest.

Deep in the wild winter wood, where the wolves
and ravens hunt, the starving wait for Spring's return
has finally come to an end.

Author's Note

Did you know ravens are also called wolf-birds? This is because of the very special relationship they have shared with wolves for what may be thousands of years. Ravens follow and steal food from wolves, and some ecologists believe wolves first formed packs to keep these persistent scavengers away.

It is also believed that ravens may lead wolves to prey. Aboriginal hunters in the US and Canada have reported seeing ravens signal to them with special calls and movements, such as wing dipping, when easy prey is nearby. The birds might attempt to draw the attention of wolves in similar ways.

Ravens need wolves—to kill for them, open tough hides, and help them past their fear of carcasses they did not see killed. Daniel Stahler, Yellowstone Wolf Project biologist, has seen wolves changing course to investigate noisy groups of ravens—only to find food sources that the birds could not eat on their own.

This connection between wolves and wolf-birds is sometimes called mutualism. This is a kind of relationship in which both living beings benefit. Other known examples of mutualism include the pistol shrimp and goby fish, and the clownfish and anemone. But when the ravens steal and wolves go hungry, this relationship is called klepto-parasitism. This means that one organism steals and benefits, while the other is harmed.

I researched and wrote *The Wolf-Birds* to celebrate the clever ways in which wolves and ravens thrive throughout the long, deadly winter. It is a story of desperation, perseverance, thievery, and occasional cooperation. It is a story of the cycle of life. I hope you enjoy it!

P.S. Please see the following page for a list of sources I consulted while making this book. For a full bibliography and a list of recommended books about wolves as a keystone species, visit www.owlkidsbooks.com.

Owlkids Books acknowledges the financial support of the Canada Council for the Arts, the Ontario Arts Council, the Government of Canada through the Canada Book Fund (CBF) and the Government of Ontario through the Ontario Media Development Corporation's Book Initiative for our publishing activities.

Published in Canada by
Owlkids Books Inc.
10 Lower Spadina Avenue
Toronto, ON M5V 2Z2

Published in the United States by
Owlkids Books Inc.
1700 Fourth Street
Berkeley, CA 94710

Cataloguing data available from Library and Archives Canada

ISBN 978-1-77147-054-4

Library of Congress Control Number: 2015900227

Edited by: John Crossingham and Karen Li
Designed by: Barb Kelly
Wolf and Raven Consultant: Daniel R. Stahler, Ph.D., Wildlife Biologist, Yellowstone Wolf Project
Research Assistant: Jalisa Henry

Manufactured in Dongguan, China, in April 2015, by Toppan Leefung Packaging & Printing (Dongguan) Co., Ltd.
Job #BAYDC14

A   B   C   D   E   F

 Publisher of Chirp, chickaDEE and OWL
www.owlkidsbooks.com

SOURCES

"A Murder of Crows." *The Nature of Things*. CBC-TV, May 5, 2014.

Dutcher, Jim, and Jamie Dutcher. *The Hidden Life of Wolves*. Washington DC: National Geographic Society, 2013.

Heinrich, Bernd. *Mind of the Raven: Investigations and Adventures with Wolf-Birds*. New York: HarperCollins, 2002.

Johnson, Sylvia A., and Alice Aamodt. *Wolf Pack: Tracking Wolves in the Wild*. Minneapolis: Lerner Publishing Group, 1985.

MacNulty, Daniel R., L. David Mech, and Douglas W. Smith. "A Proposed Ethogram of Large-Carnivore Predatory Behavior, Exemplified by the Wolf." *Journal of Mammalogy* 88.3 (2007): 595–605.

Marzluff, John M., and Tony Angell. *In the Company of Crows and Ravens*. New Haven: Yale University Press, 2005.

Mech, L. David, and Luigi Boitani. *Wolves: Behavior, Ecology, and Conservation*. Chicago: The University of Chicago Press, 2003.

Patent, Dorothy Hinshaw. *When the Wolves Returned: Restoring Nature's Balance in Yellowstone*. New York: Bloomsbury Publishing, Inc., 2008.

Stahler, Daniel R., Bernd Heinrich, and Douglas Smith. "Common ravens, *Corvus corax*, preferentially associate with grey wolves, *Canis lupus*, as a foraging strategy in winter." *Animal Behaviour* 64 (2002): 283–290.

Stahler, Daniel R. "Interspecific interactions between the common raven (*Corvus corax*) and the gray wolf (*Canis lupus*) in Yellowstone National Park, Wyoming: Investigations of a predator and scavenger relationship." M.S. thesis, University of Vermont, 2000.